THE SMILE AT THE FOOT OF THE LADDER

ALSO BY HENRY MILLER

THE
SMILE
AT
THE
FOOT
OF
####### THE
######## LADDER

by Henry Miller

A NEW DIRECTIONS BOOK

Copyright 1948 by Henry Miller
This edition first published in 1958
First issued in paper covers in 1966
This edition published as ND Paperbook 386(ISBN: 0-8112-0556-8) in 1974
Library of Congress Catalog Card No.: 58-11829

The author and publisher are grateful to the following owners of Henry Miller paintings who have made them available for reproduction in whole and in part: Willa Percival, Elena Rex, Mrs. David Karr of the Templeton Gallery and Miss Frances Steloff of the Gotham Book Mart.

Manufactured in the United States
New Directions books are printed on acid-free paper
Published in Canada by Penguin Books Canada Limited

New Directions Books are published for James Laughlin
by New Directions Publishing Corporation,
80 Eighth Avenue, New York 10011

TENTH PRINTING

THE SMILE AT THE FOOT OF THE LADDER

Nothing could diminish the lustre of that extraordinary smile which was engraved on Auguste's sad countenance. In the ring this smile took on a quality of its own, detached, magnified, expressing the ineffable.

At the foot of a ladder reaching to the moon, Auguste would sit in contemplation, his smile fixed, his thoughts far away. This simulation of ecstasy, which he had brought to perfection, always impressed the audience as the summation of the incongruous. The great favorite had many tricks up his sleeve but this one was inimitable. Never had a buffoon thought to depict the miracle of ascension.

Night in and night out he would sit thus, waiting to be nubbed by the white horse whose mane fell to the ground in rivulets of gold. The touch of the mare's warm muzzle on his neck was like the departing kiss of a loved one; it awakened him gently, as gently as the dew enlivening each blade of grass.

Within the radius of the spotlight lay the world in which he was born anew each evening. It comprised only those objects, creatures and beings which move in the circle of enchantment. A table, a chair, a rug; a horse, a bell, a paper hoop; the eternal ladder, the moon nailed to the roof, the bladder of a goat. With these Auguste and his companions managed each night to reproduce the drama of initiation and martyrdom.

Bathed in concentric circles of shadow, there rose tier upon tier of faces, broken here and there by empty spaces which the spotlight licked with the avidity of a tongue in search of a missing tooth. The musicians, swimming in dust and magnesium rays, clung to their instruments as if hallucinated, their bodies swaying like reeds in the flickering play of light and shadow. The contortionist always moved to the muffled roll of the drum, the bareback rider was always introduced with a fanfare of trumpets. As for Auguste, sometimes it was the thin squeak of a violin, sometimes the mocking notes of the clarinet, which followed him about as he capered

4

through his antics. But when the moment came to enter the trance, the musicians, suddenly inspired, would pursue Auguste from one spiral of bliss to the next, like chargers nailed to the platform of a carousel which has run wild.

Each evening, as he applied the *maquillage*, Auguste would hold a debate with himself. The seals, no matter what they were obliged to do, always remained seals. The horse remained a horse, the table a table. Whereas Auguste, while remaining a man, had to become something more: he had to assume the powers of a very special being with a very special gift. He had to make people laugh. It was not difficult to make people weep, nor even to make them laugh; he had found this out long ago, before he had ever dreamed of joining the circus. Auguste, however, had greater aspirations—he wanted to endow his spectators with a joy which would prove imperishable. It was this obsession which had originally prompted him to sit at the foot of the ladder and feign ecstasy. It was by sheer accident that he had fallen into the semblance of a trance—he had forgotten what it was he was supposed to do next. When he came to, somewhat bewildered and extremely apprehensive, he found himself being applauded wildly. The following evening he repeated the experiment, deliberately this time, praying that the senseless, raucous laughter which

5

he so easily evoked would give way to that joy supreme which he longed to communicate. But each night, despite his almost devout efforts, the same delirious applause awaited him.

The more successful it was, this little skit at the foot of the ladder, the more wistful Auguste became. Each night the laughter become more jarring to his ears. Finally it became unbearable. One night the laughter suddenly changed to jeers and cat-calls, followed by hats, refuse and more solid objects too. Auguste had failed to "come back." For thirty minutes the audience had waited; then it had grown uneasy, then suspicious, with the tension finally snapping in an explosive outburst of derision. When Auguste came to in his dressing room he was astounded to find a physician bending over him. His face and head were a mass of cuts and bruises. The blood had coagulated over the paint, distorting his image beyond recognition. He looked like something which had been abandoned on the butcher's block.

His contract abruptly terminated, Auguste fled from the world he knew. Having no desire to resume his life as a clown, he took to wandering. He drifted unknown, unrecognized, among the millions whom he had taught to laugh. There was no resentment in his heart, only a deep sadness. It was a constant fight to keep back the tears. At first he accepted this new condition of the

heart. It was nothing more, he told himself, than a malaise created by the sudden interruption of a lifelong routine. But when months had gone by he gradually came to realize that he was mourning the loss of something which had been taken from him—not the power to make people laugh, ah no! that he no longer cared about—something else, something deeper than that, something which was uniquely his own. Then one day it dawned on him that it was long, long ago since he had known the state of bliss. He trembled so upon discovering this that he could not wait to get to his room. Instead of rushing to his hotel, however, he hailed a taxi and ordered the driver to take him to the outskirts of the town. But where to exactly? the driver wanted to know. "Wherever there are trees," said Auguste impatiently. "But make haste, I beg—it's urgent."

Outside a coal yard they came upon a lone tree. Auguste ordered the driver to stop. "Is this the place?" asked the driver innocently.

"Yes, leave me in peace," responded Auguste.

For an endless time, it seemed, Auguste struggled to recreate a semblance of the mood which usually served as a prelude to the nightly performance at the foot of the ladder. Unfortunately the light was harsh: a scorching sun seared his eyeballs. "I shall just sit here," he thought to himself, "until night falls. When the moon comes out everything will fall into place." In a few moments he dozed off. It was a heavy sleep in which he dreamed that he was back again in the ring. Everything was as it had always been, except that it was no longer a circus in which things were going on. The roof had disappeared, the walls had fallen away. Above him was the real moon high in the heavens, a moon that seemed to race through stationary clouds. Instead of the usual circular tiers of benches there rose at a gentle incline, and straight to the sky, literally walls of people. Not a laugh could be heard, not a murmur. They hung there, these vast multitudes of spectres, suspended in fathomless space, each and every one of them crucified. Paralyzed with fear, Auguste forgot what it was he was

8

supposed to do. After an intolerable period of suspense, during which it seemed to him that he was more cruelly deserted and abandoned than the Saviour himself had ever been, Auguste made a frantic dash to escape the arena. But in whichever direction he ran the exits were blocked. In desperation he took to the ladder, started climbing feverishly, and climbed and climbed until his breath gave out. After due pause he ventured to open his eyes wide and look about him. First he looked downward. The foot of the ladder was almost invisible, so far below lay the earth. Then he looked upward; rung after rung stretched above him, endlessly, piercing the clouds, piercing the very blue in which the stars were cushioned. Straight to the moon rose the ladder. It was a moon which lay beyond the stars, a moon infinitely remote, glued like a frozen disk to the vault above. Auguste began to weep and then to sob. Like an echo, faint, restrained at first, but gradually swelling into an oceanic wail, there came to his ears the groans and sobs of the countless multitude which walled him about. "Horrible," muttered Auguste. "It is like birth and death at once. I am a prisoner in Purgatory." With this he swooned, falling backwards into nothingness. He regained consciousness just as he realized that the earth was pressing forward to receive him. That, he knew, would be the end of Auguste, the real end, the death of deaths. And then, like a knife gleam, there came a flash of memory. Not another second was left him; a half second, perhaps, and he would be no more. What was it that had stirred in the depths of his being, flashed like a blade, only to precede him into oblivion? He thought with such rapidity that in the fleeting fraction of a second which was left him he was able to summon up the whole pageant of his life. But the most important moment in his life, the jewel about which all the meaningful events of the past clustered, he could not revive. It was revelation itself which was foundering with him. For he knew now that at some moment in time all had been made clear to him. And now that he was about to die, this, the supreme gift, was being snatched from him. Like a miser, with a cunning and an ingenuity beyond all reckoning, Auguste succeeded in doing the impossible: seizing this last fraction of a second which had been allotted him, he began dividing it into infinitesimal moments of duration. Nothing he had experienced dur-

ing the forty years of his life, not all the moments of joy put together, could begin to compare with the sensual delight he now experienced in husbanding these splintered fragments of an exploded fraction of a second. But when he had chopped this last moment of time into infinitesimal bits, so that it spread about him like a vast web of duration, he made the alarming discovery that he had lost the power to remember. He had blanked himself out.

The following day, emotionally exhausted by the ravages of this dream, Auguste decided to remain in his room. It was only towards evening that he bestirred himself. He had spent the whole day in bed, listlessly toying with the throngs of memory which for some inexplicable reason had descended upon him like a plague of locusts. Finally, weary of being buffeted about in this vast cauldron of reminiscence, he dressed himself and sauntered out to lose himself in the crowd. It was with some difficulty that he managed to recall the name of the town through whose streets he was strolling.

At the outskirts of the town he came upon a group of circus folk, one of those fugitive bands of players who live on wheels. Auguste's heart began to beat wildly. Impulsively he rushed to one of the *roulottes*—they had been drawn up in the form of a circle—and timidly mounted the little steps which had been dropped from the rear of the vehicle. He was about to knock when the neighing of a horse close beside him arrested him. The next instant the muzzle of the horse was grazing his back. A deep joy pervaded Auguste's whole being. Putting his arms about the animal's neck, he spoke in gentle, soothing words, as if greeting a long lost friend.

The door behind him opened suddenly and a woman's voice smothered an exclamation of surprise. Startled almost out of his wits, he mumbled: "It's only me, Auguste."

"Auguste?" she repeated after him. "Don't know him."

"Excuse me," he mumbled apologetically, "I must be going."

He had gone only a few steps when he heard the woman shouting: "Hey there, Auguste, come back here! What are you running away for?"

He stopped dead, turned around, hesitated a moment, then broke into a broad grin. The woman flew towards him, arms outstretched. A mild panic seized Auguste. For a brief moment he had a notion to turn and flee. But it was too late. The woman's arms were now about him, clasping him tight.

"Auguste, Auguste!" she exclaimed over and over. "To think I didn't recognize you!"

At this Auguste paled. It was the first time in all his

wandering that any one had caught up with him. The
woman was still holding him like a vise. Now she was
kissing him, first on one cheek, then the other, then the
brow, then the lips. Auguste was quaking.

"Could I have a lump of sugar?" he begged, as soon
as he could disengage himself.

"Sugar?"

"Yes, for the horse," said Auguste.

While the woman rummaged about inside the van
Auguste made himself comfortable on the little steps.
With soft, tremulous muzzle the horse was licking the
back of his neck. It was just at this moment, strange
coincidence, that the moon shook itself clear of the distant tree tops. A wonderful calm fell upon Auguste. For
just a few seconds—it could have been hardly more than
that—he enjoyed a sort of twilight sleep. Then the
woman came bouncing out, her loose skirt brushing his
shoulder as she leapt to the ground.

"We all thought you were dead," were her first words,
as she seated herself on the grass by his feet. "The whole
world has been looking for you," she added rapidly,
passing him one lump of sugar after another.

Auguste listened mutely as the woman rattled on.
The sense of her words came to him slowly, very slowly,
as if traveling to his ears from some far distance. What
enthralled him was the delicious sensation which spread

through his body whenever the warm wet muzzle of the horse licked the palm of his hand. He was reliving intensely that intermediate stage which he used to experience nightly at the foot of the ladder, the period between the falling away of bliss and the wild burst of applause which always came to his ears like the roll of distant thunder.

Auguste never even thought of returning to the hotel to gather his few belongings. He spread a blanket on the ground beside a fire and, locked within the magic circle of wheels and wagons, he lay awake following the lurid course of the moon. When he at last closed his eyes it was with the decision to follow the troupe. He knew that he could trust them to keep his identity secret.

To help set up the tent, to roll the big rugs out, to move the props about, to water the horses and groom them, to do the thousand and one chores which were required of him, all this was sheer joy to Auguste. He lost himself with abandon in the pursuance of the menial tasks which filled his days. Now and then he indulged himself in the luxury of observing the performance as a spectator. It was with new eyes he noted the skill and the fortitude of his companions in travel. The miming of the clowns particularly intrigued him; it was a dumb show whose language was more eloquent to him now than when he was one of them. He had a sense of free-

dom which he had forfeited as a performer. O, but it was good to throw off one's role, to immerse oneself in the humdrum of life, to become as dust and yet . . . well, to know that one was still part of it all, still useful, perhaps even more useful thus. What egotism it was to imagine that because he could make men laugh and cry he was rendering them a great boon! He no longer received applause, nor gales of laughter, nor adulation. He was receiving something far better, far more sustaining —*smiles*. Smiles of gratitude? No. Smiles of recognition. He was accepted again as a human being, accepted for himself, for whatever it was that distinguished him from, and at the same time united him with, his fellow man. It was like receiving small change which, when one is in need, regenerates the heart's flow in a way that bank notes never do.

With these warm smiles which he garnered like ripe

grain each day Auguste expanded, blossomed anew. Endowed with a feeling of inexhaustible bounty, he was always eager to do more than was demanded of him. Nothing one could ask of him was too much—that was how he felt. There was a little phrase he mumbled to himself continually as he went about his tasks: "*à votre service.*" With the animals he would raise his voice, there being no need to withhold such simple words from them. "*A votre service,*" he would say to the mare, as he slipped the feed bag over her head. To the seals likewise, as he patted their gleaming backs. Sometimes, too, stumbling out of the big tent into the starlit night, he would look above as if trying to pierce the veil which protects our eyes from the glory of creation, and he would murmur softly and reverently: "*A votre service, Grand Seigneur!*"

Never had Auguste known such peace, such contentment, such deep, lasting joy. Pay days he would go to town with his meagre earnings and wander through the shops, searching for gifts to bring the children—and the animals too. For himself a bit of tobacco, nothing more.

Then one day Antoine, the clown, fell ill. Auguste was sitting in front of one of the *roulottes,* mending an old pair of trousers, when the news was brought him. He mumbled a few words of sympathy and continued with his mending. He realized immediately, of course,

16

that this unexpected event involved him. He would be asked to substitute for Antoine, no doubt about it. Auguste endeavored to quell the excitement which was rapidly mounting in him. He tried to think quietly and soberly what answer he would give when the moment came.

He waited and waited for some one to return, but no one came. No one else could take Antoine's place, he was certain of that. What was holding them back then? Finally he got up and wandered about, just to let them know he was there, that they could put the question to him whenever they wished. Still no one made effort to engage him in conversation.

At last he decided to break the ice himself. Why not, after all? Why shouldn't he volunteer his services? He felt so fortified, so full of good will towards every one. To be a clown again, it was nothing, nothing at all. He could just as well be a table, a chair, a ladder, if need be. He wanted no special privileges; he was one of them, ready to share their sorrows and misfortunes.

"Look," he said to the boss whom he had finally collared, "I'm thoroughly prepared to take Antoine's place tonight. That is," and he hesitated a moment, "unless you have some one else in mind."

"No, Auguste, there is no one else, as you know. It's good of you to offer . . ."

17

"But what?" snapped Auguste. "Are you afraid perhaps that I can no longer perform?"

"No, not that, not that. No, it would be a privilege to have you . . ."

"But what then?" demanded Auguste, almost trembling with apprehension, for he realized now that it was delicacy and tact with which he had to deal.

"Well, it's like this," the boss began in his slow, lumbering way. "You see, we've been talking it over among ourselves. We know how things are with you. Now then, if you were to take Antoine's place . . . damn it, what am I saying? Come, don't stand there looking at me like that! Look, Auguste, what I'm trying to say is . . . well, just this . . . we don't want to open old wounds. You understand?"

Auguste felt the tears rushing to his eyes. He grasped the other's two big hands, held them gently in his own and, without opening his mouth, poured out his thanks.

"Do let me take over tonight," he begged. "I'm yours as long as it's necessary—for a week, a month, six months. It will give me pleasure, that's the truth. You won't say no, hein?"

Some hours later Auguste was seated before the mirror, studying his face. It had been his habit, before applying the paint each night, to sit and stare at himself for long intervals. It was his way of preparing himself

19

for the performance. He would sit looking at his own sad face and then suddenly he would begin erasing this image and impose a new one, one which every one knew and which was accepted everywhere as Auguste. The real Auguste no one knew, not even his friends, for with fame he had become a solitary.

Seated thus, invaded by memories of thousands of other nights before the mirror, Auguste began to realize that this life apart, this life which he had jealously guarded as his own, this secret existence which supposedly preserved his identity, was not a life at all, was nothing in fact, not even a shadow life. He had only begun to live from the day he had taken up with the troupe, from the moment he had begun to serve in the capacity of the humblest. That secret life had vanished almost without his knowing it; he was a man again like other men, doing all the foolish, trifling, necessary things which others did—and he had been happy thus, his days had been full. Tonight he would appear not as Auguste, the world-celebrated clown, but as Antoine, whom nobody had heard of. Because he had neither name nor fame, Antoine was accepted each night as a matter of course. No wild applause followed his exit from the ring; people simply smiled indulgently, showing no more appreciation of his art than they did of the amazing stunts of the seals.

20

At this point a disturbing thought suddenly shattered his reverie. Heretofore it was that private, empty life which he had struggled to shield from the public eye. But what if this evening some one should recognize him, recognize the clown Auguste? That would indeed be a calamity! Never again would he have any peace; he would be pursued from town to town, pressed to explain his strange behavior, importuned to resume his proper place in the world of *vedettes*. In some vague way he sensed that they might even accuse him of murdering Auguste. Auguste had become an idol; he belonged to the world. No telling to what lengths they would go to harass him . . .

There was a knock at the door. Some one had popped in just to see if everything was going all right. After a few words Auguste inquired how Antoine was doing. "Improving, I hope?"

"No," said the other gravely, "he seems to be getting worse. No one knows just what's wrong with him. Perhaps you would say a word to him before you go on, yes?"

"Certainly," said Auguste, "I'll be with you in a few minutes," and he proceeded with his make-up.

Antoine was tossing about feverishly when Auguste entered. Bending over the sick man, Auguste took Antoine's moist hand in his. "Poor fellow," he murmured, "what can I do for you?"

Antoine stared up at him blankly for several long minutes. He was staring with the expression of one looking at himself in a mirror. Auguste slowly understood what was passing through Antoine's mind. "It's me, Auguste," he said softly.

"I know," said Antoine. "It's *you* . . . but it could also be *me*. Nobody will know the difference. And you are great and I have never been anybody."

"I was thinking that very thing myself just a few moments ago," said Auguste with a wistful smile. "It's droll, what! A little grease paint, a bladder, a funny costume—how little it takes to make oneself into a nobody! That's what we are—*nobodies*. And *everybody* at the same time. It's not us they applaud, it's themselves. My dear fellow, I must be going in a moment, but first let me tell you a little thing I learned recently. . . . To be yourself, just yourself, is a great thing. And how does one do it, how does one bring it about? Ah, that's the most difficult trick of all. It's difficult just because it involves no effort. You try neither to be one thing nor another, neither great nor small, neither clever nor maladroit . . . you follow me? You do whatever comes to hand. You do it with good grace, *bien entendu*. Because nothing is unimportant. Nothing. Instead of laugh-

ter and applause you receive smiles. Contented little smiles—that's all. But it's everything . . . more than one could ask for. You go about doing the dirty work, relieving people of their burdens. It makes them happy, but it makes *you* much happier, do you see? Of course you must do it inconspicuously, so to say. You must never let them know what pleasure it gives you. Once they catch on to you, once they learn your secret, you are lost to them. They will call you selfish, no matter how much you do for them. You can do everything for them—literally kill yourself in harness—so long as they do not suspect that they are enriching you, giving you a joy you could never give yourself. . . . Well, excuse me, Antoine, I didn't mean to make a long speech. Anyway, tonight it is you who are making me a gift. Tonight I can be myself in being you. That is even better than being yourself, *compris?*"

Here Auguste checked himself, for in giving expression to this last thought he had suddenly hit upon a genial idea. It was not one to be imparted to Antoine then and there, however. There was a certain risk involved, an element of danger possibly. But he wouldn't think of that. He must hurry now, work it out as quickly as possible . . . this very night perhaps.

23

"Look, Antoine," he said almost gruffly, making ready to leave, "I will go on tonight, and maybe tomorrow night too, but after that you had better be up and about. I'm not eager to become a clown again, you understand? I'll drop in on you in the morning. There's something more I want to tell you, something that will buck you up!" He paused a moment, cleared his throat. "You always wanted to be a big shot, didn't you? Just remember that! I'm nursing an idea: it's for you to take advantage of. So long now, sleep well!" He patted Antoine roughly, as if to push him into well-being. Moving towards the door he caught the faint suggestion of a smile stealing over Antoine's lips. He closed the door softly and tiptoed out into the darkness.

As he strode towards the big tent, humming to himself, the idea which had seized him a few moments ago began to formulate itself more distinctly. He could scarcely wait for his cue, so keen was he to bring his plan to fruition. "Tonight," he said to himself, as he stood champing at the bit, "I shall give a performance such as no one has ever seen. Just wait, my buckos, just wait till Auguste takes over."

He whipped himself into such a frenzy of impatience that when he emerged into the spotlight, accompanied by a few thin squeaks from the violin, he was cavorting like a crazy goat. From the moment his feet touched

24

the sawdust it was sheer improvisation. Not one of these wild, senseless capers had he ever thought of before, much less rehearsed. He had given himself a clean slate and on it he was writing Antoine's name in indelible letters. If only Antoine were there, could witness his own début as a world figure!

In the space of a few minutes Auguste was aware that he held the audience in the palm of his hand. And he had hardly unlimbered, so to speak. "Wait, wait, my lads!" he kept mumbling as he flung himself about, "this is nothing yet. Antoine is only just being born, he hasn't even begun to kick his legs."

The preliminary skit over, he immediately found himself surrounded by an excited group. Among them was the boss. "But you must be mad!" were the latter's first words. "Are you trying to ruin Antoine?"

"Have no fear," said Auguste, flushing with joy. "I am *making* Antoine. Be patient. I assure you all will end well."

"But it's too good already, that's what I'm growling about. After this performance Antoine will be finished."

There was no time for more words. The ring had to be cleared for the trapeze artists. As the troupe was a small one, every one had to pitch in.

When it came time for the clowns to appear again there was a prolonged burst of applause. Auguste had

25

scarcely shown his head when the audience burst into cheers. "Antoine! Antoine!" they shouted, stamping their feet, whistling, clapping their hands with joy. "Give us Antoine!"

It was at this point in the evening's entertainment that Antoine usually gave a solo performance, a rather worn little act from which the last breath of invention had evaporated years ago. Observing this routine night after night, Auguste had often thought to himself just how he would alter each little turn, were he obliged to do it himself. He now found himself executing the gags which he had so often rehearsed, sometimes in his sleep. He felt very much like a master putting the finishing touches to a portrait which a negligent pupil had abandoned. Except for the subject, there would be nothing left of the original. One began by touching it up here and there, and one ended by creating something wholly new.

Auguste went to it like an inspired maniac. There was nothing to lose. On the contrary, there was everything to

gain. Each new twist or wrinkle meant a fresh lease of life, *for Antoine*. As he proceeded to perfect the turn from one phase to the next, Auguste made mental notes to explain to Antoine exactly how to reproduce the effects he was achieving. He was hopping about like three different beings at once: Auguste the master, Auguste as Antoine, and Antoine as Auguste. And above and beyond these there hovered a fourth entity which would crystallize and become more manifest with time: Antoine as **Antoine**. A new-born Antoine, to be sure, an Antoine *in excelsis*. The more he thought of this Antoine (it was amazing how much speculation he could indulge in while holding forth) the more considerate he was of the limits and susceptibilities of the figure he was recreating. It was Antoine he kept thinking of, not Auguste. Auguste was dead. He had not the slightest desire to see him reincarnated as the world-renowned Antoine. His whole concern was to make Antoine so famous that there would nevermore be mention of Auguste.

Next morning the papers were full of Antoine's praises. Auguste had, of course, explained his project to the boss before retiring that night. It was agreed that every precaution would be taken to keep the plan a secret. Since none but the members of the troupe knew of Antoine's illness, and since Antoine himself was still in ignorance of the glorious future which had been prepared for him, the outlook seemed relatively cheerful.

Auguste, of course, could scarcely wait to pay the promised visit to Antoine. He had decided not to show him the newspapers immediately but to simply let him know what he hoped to accomplish during the few brief days in which Antoine would be incapacitated. He had to win Antoine over before revealing to him the full extent of his accomplishment, otherwise Antoine might be intimidated by a success which he had acquired ready-made. All this Auguste rehearsed step by step before heading for Antoine's quarters. Not once did it occur to him that what he was about to propose was beyond Antoine's power of acceptance.

He held himself back until almost noon, hoping that by that time Antoine would be in the proper mood to receive him. When he set forth he was jubilant. He was certain he could convince Antoine that the heritage he was leaving him was a legitimate one. "After all," he said to himself, "it's just a little push I'm giving him. Life is full of little dodges which we must avail ourselves of. No man gets there alone, unaided." With this off his chest, he almost began to trot. "I'm not cheating or robbing him," he continued. "He always wanted to be famous, now he *is* famous! or he *will* be a week from now. Antoine will be Antoine . . . only more so. That's all there is to it. All it needs sometimes is just a little

28

accident, a trick of fortune, a push from the beyond, and there you are—out in the limelight and on all fours."

Here he recalled his own sudden rise to fame. What had he, Auguste, to do with it? What had been a mere accident was acclaimed overnight as a stroke of genius. How little the public understood! How little any one understood, where fate was concerned. To be a clown was to be fate's pawn. The life in the arena was a dumb show consisting of falls, slaps, kicks—an endless shuffling and booting about. And it was by means of this disgraceful rigolade that one found favor with the public. The beloved clown! It was his special privilege to reenact the errors, the follies, the stupidities, all the misunderstandings which plague human kind. To be ineptitude itself, that was something even the dullest oaf could grasp. Not to understand, when all is clear as daylight; not to catch on, though the trick be repeated a thousand times for you; to grope about like a blind man, when all signs point the right direction; to insist on opening the wrong door, though it is marked *Danger!*; to walk head on into the mirror, instead of going around it; to look through the wrong end of a rifle, a *loaded* rifle!— people never tired of these absurdities because for millennia humans have traversed all the wrong roads, because for millennia all their seeking and questioning have landed them in a *cul-de-sac*. The master of ineptitude has all time as his domain. He surrenders only in the face of eternity. . . .

It was in the midst of such strange preoccupations that he caught sight of Antoine's *roulotte*. It startled him somewhat, though he knew not why, to observe the boss coming towards him, obviously from Antoine's bedside. He was even more startled when the boss raised his hand, motioning him to stop where he was. The expression on the man's face awakened in Auguste a distinct feeling of alarm. He stood where he was, obediently, waiting for the other to open his mouth.

When within a few feet of Auguste, the man suddenly threw up both arms in a gesture of despair and resignation. Auguste had no need to hear a word, he knew then what to expect.

"But when did it happen?" asked Auguste, after they had walked a few yards.

"Only a few minutes ago. Like that, it happened. Right in my arms."

"I don't understand," mumbled Auguste. "What *was* it that could have killed him? He was not so ill as all that last night when I spoke to him."

"Exactly," said the other.

There was something about this "exactly" which made Auguste jump.

"You don't mean . . . ?" He broke off; it was too fan-

30

tastic, he refused to harbor the thought. But the next instant he broke out with it just the same. "You don't mean," and here he faltered again, "you don't mean that he heard . . . ?"

"Precisely."

Again Auguste jumped.

"If I were asked my candid opinion," continued the boss in the same rasping tone, "I would say that he died of a broken heart."

With this they both halted abruptly.

"Look," said the boss, "it is not your fault. Don't take it too much to heart. I know, we all know, that you are innocent. In any case it's a fact that Antoine would never have made a great clown. Antoine had given up long ago." He mumbled something under his breath, then continued with a sigh: "The question is, how will we explain last night's performance? It will be hard to conceal the truth now, you agree, do you not? We never counted on his dying suddenly, did we?"

There was an interval of silence, then Auguste said quietly: "I think I would like to be alone for a while, do you mind?"

"Righto!" said the boss. "Think it out by yourself. There is still time . . ." He did not add for what.

Distraught, dejected, Auguste wandered off in the direction of the town. He walked for quite a long time with not a thought in his head, just a sort of dull, numb pain permeating his whole body. Finally he took a seat on the edge of a *terrasse* and ordered a drink. No, decidedly he had never reckoned with this eventuality. Another trick of fate. One thing was very clear—either he would have to become Auguste again or Antoine. He could no longer remain anonymous. He fell to thinking of Antoine, of the Antoine whom he had impersonated the night before. Would he be able to go through it again, this evening, with anything like the same verve and gusto? He forgot all about Antoine lying cold and dead in the wagon. Without realizing it, he had stepped into Antoine's shoes. He rehearsed the part with exactitude, analyzing it, picking it to pieces, patching it up, improving it here and there . . . he went on and on, from one turn to another, one audience to another, night after night, town after town. And then suddenly he came to. Suddenly he sat up in his seat, began talking to himself in earnest. "So you're going to become a clown again, is that it? Haven't had enough yet, eh? You killed off Auguste, you murdered Antoine . . . what next? Only two days ago you were a happy man, a free man. Now you're trapped, and a murderer to boot. And you suppose, do you, that with a guilty conscience you can make people laugh? Ah no, that's carrying it a little too far!" Auguste brought his fist down on the marble-topped table, as if to convince himself of the seriousness of his words. "A great performance last night. And why? Because no one suspected that the man who made it great was the famous Auguste. It was talent, genius, they were applauding. Not a soul could have known. Perfect. Full triumph. *And*—Q.E.D." Once again he pulled himself up, like a horse. "How's that—*Q.E.D.*? Ah, so that's it! That's why Auguste was so eager to substitute for Antoine. Auguste never cared a button whether Antoine would become great or not, did he? *Yes* or *No*? Auguste cared only to make certain that the reputation he had created really belonged to him. Auguste jumped to the bait like a fish. Bah!" He spat out a bit of saliva disgustedly.

His throat had become so parched from excitement that he clapped his hands and ordered another drink. "My God," he resumed, after he had wet his palate, "to think that a man can lay such traps for himself! Happy one day, miserable the next. What a fool! What a fool I am!" Here he reflected a moment very soberly. "Well, there's one thing I understand now—my happiness was real but unfounded. I have to recapture it, but honestly this time. I have to hold on to it with two hands, as

though it were a precious jewel. I must learn to be happy as Auguste, as the clown that I am."

He took another sip of wine, then shook himself like a dog. "Maybe this is my last chance, I shall start from the bottom once more." With this he fell to speculating on a new name for himself. This game took him far afield. "Yes," he resumed, having forgotten already the name he had decided on, "I'll work out something new, something totally new. If it doesn't make me happy it will at least keep me on the alert. Perhaps South America. . . ."

The resolution to begin afresh was so strong that he almost galloped back to the fair grounds. He went at once in search of the boss.

"It's decided," he said breathlessly, "I'm leaving right now. I'm going away, far away, where nobody will possibly know me. I'm going to begin all over again."

"But why?" exclaimed the big one. "Why do you have to start afresh when you've already established a great reputation?"

"You won't understand but I'll tell you just the same. *Because I want to be happy this time.*"

"*Happy?* I don't understand. Why happy?"

"Because usually a clown is happy only when he is

somebody else. I don't want to be anybody but myself."

"Don't understand a word of it....Listen, Auguste..."

"Look," said Auguste, wringing his hands, "what makes people laugh and cry when they watch us?"

"My dear fellow, what has all that to do with it? Those are academic questions. Let's talk sense. Let's get down to reality."

"That's what I've just discovered," said Auguste gravely. "*Reality!* that's the very word for it. Now I know who I am, what I am, and what I must do. *That's reality*. What you call reality is sawdust; it crumbles away, slips through the fingers."

"My dear Auguste," the other began, as if pleading with a lost one, "you've been thinking too much. If I were you I'd go back to town and have a good snort. Don't try to make a decision now. Come . . ."

"No," said Auguste firmly, "I want no consolation, nor advice. My mind is made up." And he held out his hand in parting.

"As you like," said the big fellow, humping his shoulders. "So it's good-bye, is it?"

"Yes," said Auguste, "it's good-bye . . . forever."

Once again he started out into the world, into its very bowels this time. Approaching the town, it came over him that he had not more than a few sous in his pocket. In a few hours he would be hungry. Then it would grow

35

cold and then, like the beasts in the field, he would fold up and lie waiting for the first rays of the sun.

Why he had chosen to walk through the town, pursuing every street to the end, he knew not. He might just as well have conserved his strength.

"And if I do get to South America one day . . . ?" (He had begun talking aloud to himself.) "It may take years. And what language will I speak? And why will they take me, a stranger and unknown? Who knows if they even have a circus in such places. If they do, they will have their own clowns and their own language."

Coming to a little park, he flung himself on a bench. "This has to be thought out more carefully," he cautioned himself. "One doesn't rush off to South America just like that. I'm not an albatross, by God! I'm Auguste, a man with tender feet and a stomach that needs to be filled." One by one he began to specify all the very human attributes which distinguished him, Auguste, from the birds of the air and the creatures of the deep. His ruminations finally tailed off in a prolonged consideration of those two qualities, or faculties, which most markedly separate the world of humans from the animal kingdom—laughter and tears. Queer, he thought to himself, that he who was at home in this realm should be speculating on the subject like a schoolboy.

"*But I'm not an albatross!*" This thought, certainly

not a brilliant one, kept repeating itself as he revolved his dilemma backwards and forwards. If not original or brilliant, it was nevertheless very comforting, very reassuring to Auguste, this idea that not by any possible stretch of the imagination could he regard himself as an albatross.

South America—what nonsense! The problem was not where to go or how to get there, the problem was. . . . He tried to put it to himself very very simply. Wasn't it just this, that perhaps he was all right just as he was—without diminishing or augmenting himself? The mistake he had made was to go beyond his proper bounds. He had not been content to make people laugh, he had tried to make them joyous. Joy is God-given. Had he not discovered this in abandoning himself—by doing whatever came to hand, as he once put it?

Auguste felt that he was getting somewhere. His real tragedy, he began to perceive, lay in the fact that he was unable to communicate his knowledge of the existence of another world, a world beyond ignorance and frailty, beyond laughter and tears. It was this barrier which kept him a clown, God's very own clown, for truly there was no one to whom he could make clear his dilemma.

And then and there it came to him—how simple it was!—that to be nobody or anybody or everybody did not prevent him from being himself. If he were really a

clown, then he should be one through and through, from the time he got up in the morning until he closed his eyes. He should be a clown in season and out, for hire or for the sheer sake of being. So unalterably convinced was he of the wisdom of this that he hungered to begin at once—without make-up, without costume, without even the accompaniment of that squeaky old violin. He would be so absolutely himself that only the truth, which now burned in him like a fire, would be recognizable.

Once again he closed his eyes, to descend into darkness. He remained thus a long time, breathing quietly and peacefully on the bed of his own being. When he

finally opened his eyes he beheld a world from which the veil had been removed. It was the world which had always existed in his heart, ever ready to manifest itself, but which only begins to beat the moment one beats in unison with it.

Auguste was so utterly moved that he could not believe his eyes. He rubbed the back of his hand across them, only to discover that they were still wet with the tears of joy which he had shed unknowingly. Bolt upright he sat, with eyes staring straight ahead, struggling to accustom sight to vision. From the depths of his being there issued an incessant murmur of thanks.

He rose from the bench just as the sun was suffusing

39

the earth with a last flush of gold. Strength and longing surged through his veins. New-born, he took a few steps forward into the magical world of light. Instinctively, just as a bird takes wing, he threw out his arms in an all-encompassing embrace.

The earth was swooning now in that deep violet which ushers in the twilight. Auguste reeled in ecstasy. "At last, at last!" he shouted, or thought he shouted, for in reality his cry was but a faint reverberation of the immense joy which rocked him.

A man was coming towards him. A man in uniform and armed with a club. To Auguste he appeared as the angel of deliverance. Auguste was about to throw himself into the arms of his deliverer when a cloud of darkness felled him like a hammer blow. He crumpled at the officer's feet without a sound.

Two bystanders who had witnessed the scene came running up. They knelt down and turned Auguste over on his back. To their amazement he was smiling. It was a broad, seraphic smile from which the blood bubbled and trickled. The eyes were wide open, gazing with a candor unbelievable at the thin sliver of a moon which had just become visible in the heavens.

EPILOGUE

EPILOGUE

OF ALL the stories I've written this is perhaps the most singular. It was expressly written for Fernand Léger, to accompany a series of forty illustrations on clowns and circuses.*

It took me months, after I had accepted Léger's invitation to do the text, to even begin. Though I was given complete liberty, I felt inhibited. Never before had I written a story to order, as it were.

Almost obsessively my mind kept revolving about these names: Rouault, Miro, Chagall, Max Jacob, Seurat. I almost wished I had been asked to do the illustrations instead of the text. In the past I had made a few water

---

* Léger was obliged to reject my text as unsuitable and subsequently wrote one himself for his handsome book called *Le Cirque*.

43

colors of clowns, one of them called "Cirque Medrano."
At least one of these clowns resembles strongly Marc
Chagall, I am told, though I have never met Chagall
nor had I even seen a photograph of him.

While struggling to get started, there fell into my
hands a little book by Wallace Fowlie* in which there
is a poignant essay on the clowns of Rouault. Meditat-
ing on Rouault's life and work, which influenced me
strongly, I got to thinking of the clown which I am,
which I have always been. I thought of my passion for
the circus, especially the *cirque intime,* and how all
these experiences as spectator and silent participator
must lie buried deep in my consciousness. I remembered
how, when I was graduating from High School, they had
asked me what I intended to be and I had said—"a
clown!" I recalled how many of my old friends were
like clowns in their behavior—and they were the ones
I loved most. And later on I discovered to my surprise
that my most intimate friends looked upon *me* as a
clown.

And then suddenly I realized what an impact the title
of Wallace Fowlie's book (the first of his I read) had
made upon me: *Clowns and Angels.* Balzac had spoken
to me of the angels (in *Louis Lambert*) and, through

---

* *Jacob's Night,* by Wallace Fowlie: Sheed & Ward, N. Y. 1947.

Fowlie's numerous divagations on the clown, I had gained new insight into the role of the clown. Clowns and angels are so divinely suited to one another.

Moreover, had I not myself written somewhere about August Angst and Guy le Crêvecœur? Who were they, these two anguished, frustrated, desperate souls, if not myself?

And then another thing . . . the most successful painting I ever did was the head of a clown to whom I had given two mouths, one for joy and one for sorrow. The joyous mouth was in high vermilion—it was a singing mouth. (Recalling this, I realized that I no longer sang!)

Between times I received a few *maquettes* from Léger. One of them featured the head of a horse. I put these away in a drawer, forgot about them, and began to write. I never realized until I had finished the story where I got the horse. The ladder, of course, was a gift from Miro, and the moon too, most likely. (*Dog Barking at the Moon* was the first Miro I ever saw.)

I began then with myself, with the firm conviction that I had in me all there was to know about clowns and circuses. I wrote from line to line, blindly, not knowing what would come next. I had myself; the ladder and the horse I had unconsciously filched. Keeping me company were the poets and painters I adored—Rouault, Miro, Chagall, Max Jacob, Seurat. Curiously, all these artists are poet and painter both. With each one of them I had deep associations.

A clown is a poet in action. He *is* the story which he enacts. It is the same story over and over—adoration, devotion, crucifixion. "A Rosy Crucifixion," *bien entendu.*

The only part of my narrative which gave me difficulty were the last few pages, which I rewrote several times. "There is a light which kills," I believe Balzac said somewhere. I wanted my protagonist, Auguste, to go out like a light. But not in death! I wanted his death to illumine the way. I saw it not as an end but as a beginning. When Auguste becomes himself life begins—and not just for Auguste but for all mankind.

Let no one think that I thought the story out! I have told it only as I felt it, only as it revealed itself to me piece by piece. It is mine and it is not mine. Undoubtedly it is the strangest story I have yet written. It is not a Surrealistic document, not the least. The process of writing it may have been Surrealistic, but that is only to say that the Surrealists recaptured the true method of creation. No, more even than all the stories which I based on fact and experience is this one truth. My whole aim in writing has been to tell the truth, as I know it. Heretofore all my characters have been real, taken from life, my own life. Auguste is unique in that he came from the blue. But what is this blue which surrounds and envelopes us if not reality itself? We invent nothing, truly. We borrow and recreate. We uncover and discover. All has been given, as the mystics say. We have only to open our eyes and hearts, to become one with that which is.

The clown appeals to me deeply, though I did not always know it, precisely because he is separated from the world by laughter. His is never a Homeric laughter. It is a silent, what we call a mirthless, laughter. The clown teaches us to laugh at ourselves. And this laughter of ours is born of tears.

Joy is like a river: it flows ceaselessly. It seems to me that this is the message which the clown is trying to convey to us, that we should participate through ceaseless flow and movement, that we should not stop to reflect, compare, analyze, possess, but flow on and through, endlessly, like music. This is the gift of surrender, and the clown makes it symbolically. It is for us to make it real.

At no time in the history of man has the world been so full of pain and anguish. Here and there, however, we meet with individuals who are untouched, unsullied, by the common grief. They are not heartless individuals, far from it! They are emancipated beings. For them the world is not what it seems to us. They see with other

47

eyes. We say of them that they have died to the world. They live in the moment, fully, and the radiance which emanates from them is a perpetual song of joy.

The circus is a tiny closed off arena of forgetfulness. For a space it enables us to lose ourselves, to dissolve in wonder and bliss, to be transported by mystery. We come out of it in a daze, saddened and horrified by the everyday face of the world. But the old everyday world, the world with which we imagine ourselves to be only too familiar, is the only world, and it is a world of magic, of magic inexhaustible. Like the clown, we go through the motions, forever simulating, forever postponing the grand event. We die struggling to get born. We never were, never are. We are always in process of becoming, always separate and detached. Forever outside.

This is the picture of August Angst, alias Guy le Crêvecœur—or the everyday face of the world, with two mouths. Auguste is of another breed. Perhaps I have not limned his portrait too clearly. But he exists, if only for the reason that I imagined him to be. He came from the blue and he returns to the blue. He has not perished, he is not lost. Neither will he be forgotten. Only the other day I was speaking to a painter I know about the figures left us by Seurat. I said that they were rooted there where he gave them being—eternally. How grateful I am to have lived with these figures of Seurat—on the Grande Jatte, at the Medrano, and elsewhere in the mind! There is nothing in the least illusory about these creations of his. Their reality is imperishable. They dwell in sunlight, in a harmony of form and rhythm which is sheer melody. And so with the clowns of Rouault, the angels of Chagall, the ladder and the moon of Miro, his whole menagerie, in fact. So with Max Jacob, who never ceased to be a clown, even after he had found God. In word, in image, in act, all these blessed souls who kept me company have testified to the eternal reality of their vision. Their everyday world will one day become ours. It is ours now, in fact, only we are too impoverished to claim it for our own.

Henry Miller

SOME BOOKS BY HENRY MILLER
published by NEW DIRECTIONS

THE AIR-CONDITIONED NIGHTMARE
An account of a three-year trip through the United States.
Paperbound

ALLER RETOUR NEW YORK
An exuberant, humorous account of a visit to New York in 1935
and return to Europe aboard a Dutch ship. Hardbound and
paperbound.

BIG SUR AND THE ORANGES OF
HIERONYMUS BOSCH
Henry Miller here describes the earthly paradise he found on the
California coast and the devils, human and natural, which have
threatened it. Paperbound.

THE BOOKS IN MY LIFE
A candid and self-revealing journey back into memory, sharing
with the reader the thrills of new discovery that a life-time of
wide reading has brought to an original and questioning mind.
Paperbound.

THE COLOSSUS OF MAROUSSI
A travel book about Greece. "It gives you a feeling of the country
and the people that I have never gotten from any modern book."
(Edmund Wilson.) Paperbound.

THE COSMOLOGICAL EYE
A miscellany of representative examples of Miller stories,
sketches, prose poems, philosophical and critical essays, sur-
realist fantasies, and autobiographical notes. Included are
several sections from *Black Spring*, together with the famous
story "Max." Paperbound.

A DEVIL IN PARADISE
"...the work of a great novelist *manqué*, a novelist who has
no stricter sense of form than the divine creator." — *The Times
Literary Supplement* (London). Paperbound.

INTO THE HEART OF LIFE: HENRY MILLER
   AT ONE HUNDRED
In celebration of the centennial of his birth, a captivating selec-
tion of writing from ten of Miller's books. Edited by Frederick
Turner. Paperbound.

JUST WILD ABOUT HARRY
This tragicomic slapstick "melo-melo in seven scenes" is Miller's
only excursion into playwriting—the simple story of a heartless
Harry (the one the ladies are wild about) who learns a bittersweet
lesson about life, death, and love.

LETTERS TO EMIL
Correspondence from 1921 through 1924 with Miller's boyhood
friend and successful artist Emil Schnellock. A compelling
record of the writer in the making. Hardbound and paperbound.

THE NIGHTMARE NOTEBOOK
Facsimile journal of Miller's American travels. Limited to 700
copies, this extraordinary reproduction is signed and numbered
by the author. There are included twenty-two illustrated pages
printed in both full and partial color.

STAND STILL LIKE THE HUMMINGBIRD
A collection of stories and essays, many of which have appeared
only in foreign magazines or in small limited editions now out of
print, reflecting the incredible vitality and variety of interests
of Henry Miller. Hardbound and paperbound.

THE TIME OF THE ASSASSINS
A study of Rimbaud that is as much a study of Miller and
has throughout the electric quality of miraculous empathy.
Paperbound.

THE WISDOM OF THE HEART
A rich collection of Miller's stories and philosophical pieces,
including his studies of D. H. Lawrence and Balzac. Paperbound.

THE DURRELL-MILLER LETTERS, 1935-1980
Correspondence between Lawrence Durrell and Henry Miller.
Edited by Ian S. MacNiven. Hardbound.

FROM YOUR CAPRICORN FRIEND
The best of letters, drawings, and prose pieces contributed
by Miller in 1978-80, the last three years of his life, to the
New York little magazine, the *Stroker*. Paperbound.

THE HENRY MILLER READER
A cross-section designed to show the whole range of Miller's writ-
ing—stories, literary essays, "portraits" of people and places—
interlarded with new autobiographical comments by Henry
Miller. Edited, with an introduction, by Lawrence Durrell.
Paperbound.

HENRY MILLER ON WRITING
Passages on the art and practice of writing chosen from all
of Miller's books, brought together by Thomas H. Moore,
co-founder of the Henry Miller Literary Society, with Miller's
active collaboration. Paperbound.

New Directions Paperbooks—A Partial Listing

For complete listing request free catalog from
New Directions, 80 Eighth Avenue, New York 10011

†Biling